THE DICHOTOMY PROJECT

by
Michael T. Leslie and Alison Craven Roberts

Order this book online at www.trafford.com
or email orders@trafford.com

Most Trafford titles are also available at major online book retailers.

Printed in Victoria, BC, Canada.

ISBN: 978-1-4269-1952-7 (sc)
ISBN: 978-1-4269-1953-4 (hc)

Library of Congress Control Number: 2009937627

Our mission is to efficiently provide the world's finest, most comprehensive book publishing service, enabling every author to experience success. To find out how to publish your book, your way, and have it available worldwide, visit us online at www.trafford.com

Trafford rev. 12/03/09

Trafford
PUBLISHING® www.trafford.com

North America & international
toll-free: 1 888 232 4444 (USA & Canada)
phone: 250 383 6864 ♦ fax: 812 355 4082

dī-kŏt'ə-mē:

Division into two usually contradictory parts or opinions

Preface

This book of poetry that you are holding in your hands is the result of a conversation we had one weekend about various themes in poetry. As we discussed the topic a light bulb went off and we realized that we had hit upon a great idea for the book that became The Dichotomy Project.

However, we quickly found collaboration very difficult (we are cousins after all), because our viewpoints are so divergent. We soon realized, however, that this divergence created an interesting push-pull affect when we put our poetry together. This dichotomy became the very heart of our work.

In writing this volume of poetry we overcame many obstacles including a six-month separation, working in partnership over the Internet, and telephone.

We have both enjoyed the great adventure in writing this book, and have become a bit closer. We hope you have as much fun reading this book as we had writing it.

Yes we still disagree (we are family after all).

Regards,

Alison Craven Roberts
Michael T. Leslie

To my parents, Robert and Marion and my sister Joye, gone but never far in my heart. And all those who have taught me how to appreciate the simple miracle that is life. To all those who were wounded or gave their lives in the sands of Iraq and to the family and friend they left behind. And last, but never least to my partner in crime, you are always there when I need you most, Alison.

-- Michael

To my grandmother, whom I remember every time I pick up a hook or a pen. To my parents who believe in me even when they don't understand what I'm doing, and to my husband Mike for truly being my biggest fan. And lastly to Michael, for being my co-conspirator, my counselor, my confidante, and my friend. ------------

--Alison

To Mike for putting up with us both during this project.

--Alison and Michael

Table of Contents

LOSS

The Lost

How long has it been now?
How long has it been?
Since I felt your arms around me?
Since I held you close?
So frail, and yet so strong;
You always were a contradiction.
Modest and secretive,
Perhaps to a fault,
But I loved you.
I still do.
A stoic by nature,
You hid yourself well.
But we all knew
By the lingering hugs,
not merely polite,
and the ten-dollar bills
Discretely slipped into pockets and purses.
It became a game to you.
Now the games are over,
I wouldn't call myself the winner,
'Cause in the end,
I lost you to God

Riding The Storm

This poem is dedicated with a son's love to his mother

I went to Colorado after my mother died.
I failed in my honor to be at her bedside.
Instead, I chose my military duty at Fort Hood.
Yet, there at her graveside with my family I stood.

All my family thought that I was insane.
How could I ever begin to explain?
I wanted to escape my sorrow and shame.
I wanted to be alone with God and my pain.

I wanted to feel joy, to be high and alive.
I wanted something to fight for, to strive.
I wanted to laugh, to cry, to just be.
I wanted to run mad through the valley.

I wanted to scream and shout at the sky.
I wanted to ride a horse, make it fly
Over fallen trees and brush-choked trails narrow,
Through rain-swollen rivers into rocky grottos.

I yelled and jumped clear, when the horse fell.
Rain splattered around me in this chilly gray hell
Lightning tore a jagged scar across the dark sky.
A little that day I died, and in the rain I cried.

I remembered her smile, her advice, her grace.
I remembered the tears falling down her face,
The day I told her I had joined the Army.
"My boy is a man" is what she told me.

I remember her reading to me when I had to flu
Adventures in books shared only by us two.
I remember her telling me to spit into life's storm.
To scream: "Do your worst, I shall fear no harm!"

I remembered of her most, her spirit burning bright.
Always there, guiding me through darkest night.
The brooding thunder resounded and around me echoed.
The horse rose, I mounted and into the storm rode.

I smiled through the stinging downpour and hail
I remembered the golden rule of the proving trail:
"You ride the trail no matter how rugged or tough,
When the going gets rough, you gotta cowboy up."

FREEDOM

Prison

Not every prison is made of bars.
Some are made of walls
And desks, and chairs, and computers
And bosses who say one thing
And do another.
With rules you don't know about
Until they are broken
And firing threats
For the breaking,
And unprovoked fits, in which
Your dignity is stripped away;
Fit by fit, and day by day.
Yet you stay.
For the bills to pay…
And the desk, and the walls—
They were all you ever wanted,
You never wanted much.
So they pay a shiny penny
And you pay them with your soul.
And you ask yourself
"Why do I stay?"
And you answer, " For the bills to pay"
Ain't that the way?

Bound by Society's Chains

Go to your room!
You're under arrest.
Halt! Go no further.
Authority's voice booms,
Right outside your door.
I alone cannot resist
Can you sister or brother?
Run? No. The way is barred.

Bound by society's chains
Heedless of senseless pain
We each endure the shame
When to all the truth is plain
Do you need me to explain
That which you should know?
Then listen up dawg, pal, amigo
You too senorita, sista, girlfriend
Before we take the big dirt nap end.
Or into that bright light we all go.

Curse our Puritan forefathers
Who landed on that damn rock
Who first said: "Thou shall not."
Oh what a pity! What a shock!

When in Europe it is so natural
This blissful heaven they enjoy
Learning to touch, to love and trust
Learning of sweet passion and lust
Exploring each other, girl and boy
This simplest of all life's blissful joys.

The caress, the kiss, the treasured orgasm
Leaving lovers bodies weak, happy, a spasm
Embracing entangled, in silken sheets and dreams
Asleep in each other's arms, far from harsh reality
An Adam, an Eve, lost they are in passion's storm
They comprehend neither measure of fear or harm.

Nor bound are they by any of society's chains
They touch, caress and kiss with no sin or shame
Nor do they suffer any Puritan inspired guilt or pain
To their parents they simply have no need to explain.
Their emotions run rampant as a hangman's mob.
As George Foreman put it: "People, we've been robbed."

LOVE

Love

A spark
Magnetism
A flame
A raging fire of passion
A comforting warmth
Of hand-holding
Nuzzling and caressing
An empowering force
A consuming inferno
A re-birth of the soul
A death of the self
An endless contradiction.

Love's Vulnerability

Woman from a distant tropic island
I want to hold you, then hand in hand
At sunset walk along a secluded beach
Prints vanishing into sea finger's reach
No thinking or planning beyond today.
Not wondering what in the future lay.
In our heaven stay with me this one day.

Allow me to in your island beauty bask.
Hold me, know me, take me not to task.
Your hair is the sea reflecting the night
Smooth skin tanned with golden lights.
Black pearl eyes, glowing sagely and wise
Seeing the world from an innocent guise
Soft rose lips whose bliss I so long to kiss.
Fingers delving to hear pleasure's soft hiss
Curves, legs and breasts I wish to adore.
Fingers and lips impatient to all explore.
Running my fingers through you dark hair
There is no woman to you that can compare
Heaven is found holding you in my arms
Locked together, riding passion's frenzied storm
Hell is waking in the dark to find myself alone.

You scare me because never have I felt so weak
As when after talking to you I hang up the phone.
Your scare me because never have I felt so strong
As when I hear your voice and the shadows recede.
Love is all-consuming heat that only you can feed.
My body is your realm; you rule my fragile heart.
I feel you with me no matter how near or how far.
No matter where ever you are, I am there with you.
Cursed I was one and alone, then God sent me you.
You are my sunrise, my moonset, my heart's treasure.
On all this earth there is absolutely no way to measure
Nothing in all my adventures, journeys and my travels

Prepared me for the truth that leaves me here unraveled
More bare and unclothed, than I have ever felt before.
Long I will wait for you, the other side of destiny's door.
Without you I suffer knowing no life, no peace, nor rest.
You are a passionate storm that leaves me breathless,
Castaway upon the sandy reaches of a foreign shore.
Black Pearl come to my arms and let you me adore.
The truth that we run and run from a child could see
My lady there is only me for you, you for me.

PERCEPTION

I Get the World

You stride around
Your cloudless world
Refuse to hear the thunder,
Heedless of the falling the rain
Until you're swept away.

Your world is of eternal spring
You blind yourself to barren trees
Your sandaled feet can't feel
The snow as you sink deep;
Though frostbite erodes your toes,
You insist it is sand.

So my world is not a timeless green
With cloudless sky, perpetual sun.
I see the falling leaves
I hear the thunder and the rain.
I feel the cold wind
And snow upon my frozen cheeks.

I get the world:
Hot, cold, green, red, brown,
Wet, dry,
Gritty, raw, and real.
I get the world,
Not a plastic imitation.

Perception

Perception

Do you see the changes you've made?
Do you feel the hammer and chisel in your hand?
You mold and shape me like an artist working in clay.
Thank you my lady, for making me more than a mere mortal man.

Perception

If only I could learn to view myself as you do.
Loan me your eyes so I may recognize.
Myself, in all the many smiles and guises
That I wear the long day through.

Perception

Stopping for a moment on a street corner attention to pay
As I have never done before in light of this new dawning day.
Seeing all about me with virgin eyes from your point of view
This Real World as only you can do.
Not in horrid black and white, or bleary washed-out gray.
But in multitudes of Spring and Summer hues;
Followed by Autumn and Winter shades.

Perception

No matter how many countries you have seen, nor how far you have
traveled;
No matter how many ancient tomb's secrets and mysteries you have
unraveled.
There is for all viewing, looking and seeing one rule.
Where perception is concerned there can only be one universal truth.

Perception is only true
As long as you always remember to remain you.

Perception

SIBLINGS

To My Sister

I have loved you
And I've hated you
Sometimes not knowing which
When the memories of our childhood play
Were overshadowed by
That overwhelming sense
That I could never be quite as good.
You gave me something to strive for.

When I was 5, I stole your schoolbooks.
Do you remember that?
Hell-bent on being just as smart,
Though you had a 4-year head start.

When I was 10, I finally beat you at something,
As if puberty were an achievement,
Only to learn my victory hollow,
Discomfort my only prize.

When I was 15, I aimed again.
This time, I'd be the level-headed one.
I'd pass my test, and earn my wings,
Only to find that wasn't my only tether.

When I was 22, I had to quit the game.
The competition that ensnared me
Had no place for you.
My own body the enemy.

At some point I looked back
And I saw our roads diverged.
I was never chasing after you.
I was running my own race.

Gazing upon your daughter's shining face,
I know you've won yours.
And 31 years wiser
I can cheer for you.

My darling Joye

Perhaps it is your father or mother.
Maybe it is that sister or brother?
Cause there is absolutely no other
That could drive you so insane.
With one phone call from so far away
Reach out and ruin your awesome day.
Sisters are the worst! Let me tell you boy.
They rule brothers' lives as if they were toys.

In my case, there was my only sister, My Darlin' Joye.

One girl against her four brothers stood.
Hah, no way was she going to manage this brood.
The war was on! We did all we could (yeah right!).
She could out run, out fish, out hunt, and out fight,
She did it all in pure sisterly glee, meanness and spite.
Bruised and battered, we four never even had a chance
Against this tiny tower of determined feminine might.
And If I did complain, she would only wag her finger and smile:
"Remember Michael Todd, I wiped, powdered and diapered your butt."
Leaving me gagging for a retort (male ego shattered), blushing neon red.
"That makes me not only your sister and I'm practically your second Mom."
To which as all wise men know beyond their years, there is simply no reply.
Only sisters can make you want to just run away and just die!

Oh Thank God, I suffer under only one sister, my darlin' Joye.

As I grew older I discovered the most amazing of creatures.
They had long legs, wore skirts and their hair fell in curls!
They looked at me, smiled, winked and whispered behind hands.
Then in one quick pack they darted, skipping away, all giggling.
Heart pounding, I ran for home. What do I do? What do I do?
One even whispered in my ear and asked me to the spring prom!
Yes! Today I am man! Able to leap buildings in a single bound!
Wait! Wait a minute, I forgot something. Yikes, I can't dance!
No. No way! I have only her to help in this most dire circumstance.
Lord God, are you laughing at me as I muster the courage to ask?
Smirking that I'm-your-all-knowing-older-sister-smirk, she taught me.
She never complained when a hundred times I stepped on her toes.

A suit she bought me, respect she taught me, yeah and about roses too.
When I came home, laughing, she waited and wrestled me to the ground.
Every magic moment she made me reveal or she'd pound and pound.

No sister could hit as hard as my darlin' Joye.

Now I am older and seen much of the world, both here and abroad.
As a man I struggle to comprehend the gray void of life's daily fog.
Funny how time and distance, those thieves of family and friends,
Can sneak up, snatching away all that would have or might have been.
But I can certainly tell you whose stamp upon my person I feel this day.
As I stand here with my brothers, silent, proud, each holding tears at bay.
Low we laid her, in eternal slumber and peace and sped her on her way.
I stand alone at her side, with a lingering regret from which there is no
escape.
No. There is no escaping whose hand raised me up to man from boy.

Lord, how I love you, how I will miss you my darlin' Joye.

INSPIRATION

I Want to Be

I want to be
That beauty you see in me
Peering into my face
In the night's wee hours
When the make-up is gone
And I know what I would see
If I dared look in the mirror.

I want to be
That mind you see in me
When you let me explain something to you
Like I'm the world's most wise
Though it seems so small
Yet, I'm not patronized.

I want to be
That heart you see in me
The one that gives of itself
With no thought of me,
Selfless and pure of motive
A pillar of charity,
Though I swear you'd do the same.

I want to be
That strength you see in me
When I endure a hardship
Before your eyes
With no tears on my face
Though there are plenty I hide.

I want to be
All that you see in me:
The brilliant mind you swear I have
The largest heart you've ever seen
The strongest will you've ever known.

That impossible perfection.

I Am a Candle

I am a candle burning bright.
A beacon shining throughout the night
Of parents' hopes and parents' dreams
Heir apparent to all their youthful fantasies it seems.
Yet I am me.
I will be who I choose to be.

I long to travel to distant lands
To tread my way across Time's hourglass sands.
Please, Father understand
Your young son is now a man.

I have my own wishes and my own dreams.
Sparkling before me like endless streams.
I am still your son, aflame with the life you gave me,
Standing ready to meet and conquer my destiny.

To fill the waiting world with my wit and prose,
My own form of beauty as that of a spring rose.
I am young with much to learn.
How for excitement and adventure I yearn!

London, Rome, Athens, Berlin and Paris!
Cities full of romance and promise.
But no matter where I wander I know
That I still have time to learn and grow
I will see them all under the stars at night.
I am a candle burning bright!

HERITAGE

The Blanket Weaver

I watch her hands with the needles
Over and through
Over and through
As her story is knitted in a simple row of white
Her hands tell the stories
Of a suffering age
Of a loving heart
Of the fiercest will
The yarn comes together to show her to me
Her life
Her laughter
Her heartache
Her love
Each inch of yarn folded and twisted to be
Her happiness
Her sorrow
Her strength
Her weakness
And now her arms no longer enfold me
Her needles are still and her hands are silent
But her life wraps around me
As I huddle beneath it
And it keeps me from cold
As she would have done
Her life in every stitch
Every row
Every turn
Every knot
Every little imperfection.
And so she will live on in me.

In a Scottish Glen Here I Stand

By descent I was born an American
By blood and heritage, I am a Scot
So here I stand in the quiet of the glen
A solitary man, alone with his thought

Remembering those tales of heroes and rogues
Of William Wallace, the outlaw Rob Roy
And Bonnie Prince Charlie; all Scots of old
Who live in myth and legends told to wee boys

Tales that stir the heritage, pulling me toward a home
I come to remember those ancestors of the clan blood
Somewhere I have never been, yet somehow belong
Highwaymen, pirates, and soldiers; here each has stood

Arise my distant kinsman! Let us share a drink or two
It is all true what I've read in the family histories?
Let me see the kilt, our coat of arms and speak to you.
Share with me a pipe, some stew and spin me a story.

What was it like here when you were all around?
I wish to understand the land upon which you grew.
I long to touch the past, to feel that I have found
Some lost connection to a family that I never knew.

To hear the sweet melancholy of highland pipes played,
When my kinsman did battle with the army of a tyrant king
Across the moors, vales and lochs recalling those glory days,
In their quiet places, the little Sith dance the reel and sing

To the ancient land nourished by the clan's soul and blood.
Rest you well my distant cousins for I will come to visit again
When the demands of what I would do, could and should do
Have swallowed me whole and dragged me down the drain

When I need to escape this fast-food world of progress and steel
To recall the stillness of the loch upon a mist-shrouded morn,
Lost in the cold void, to stop and sense, to be and to feel.
To hear past glories heralded with the call of the highland horn.

Recalling fireside yarns and tales told in snowy December.
Pausing for a brief wishful, moment to listen and remember.
I am no longer an American cousin but one amidst the clan.
Aye, for that moment, here in a Scottish glen I stand.

PERSEVERENCE

Powerless

Shot through the head
I barely can stand.
My body longs to stagger and fall
But my mind perseveres.

Full of questions my lips cannot ask
I feel life bleeding away
And wonder why. And how.
And when it will end.

I no longer have control
My life has slipped through my fingers
Ruled now by pain and confusion.
I am powerless,
And I know it.
But I have to go on.

Yo' Girl

Yo, Girl! Yeah, you there.
Thinking your life is done; you got nowhere to go.
Get up off your ass. Get on your way
Cause you aren't ready to die, not this day.

You can forget and let go that lonely knife.
Now, I know that all your young sorry life
You've known nothing, but pain, strife and sorrow
But I promise you girl there will be a tomorrow.

Well girl I am the hand reaching down through the dark waters.
I am the friend and man to show you a new border.
A line has been drawn in your life's hourglass sands.
Not by me, but by your very own hand.

Now girl I am here to tell you the truth.
You want that good life, man, and solid roof?
Don't let yourself be no man's slut, no crack whore or tool.
Laugh in the faces of all those bastards who called you fool.

Life threw you down and kicked you in the teeth
They buried you deep in crystal meth, beyond all reach
You gonna just lay there and die in this hazy grave?
Or you gonna rise up and make them muthers pay?

Thought you were a scrapper, so Bitch,
Climb your way out of that bottomless abyss.
Fight, girl, hit, kick and scream, cause you ain't nearly through.
Make those muthers sorry that they ever met you!

Take up your paper and pen.
Tell those bastards that this is your beginning, not your end.
Fight the darkness inside with your weapons of choice.
Let the world hear your glorious scrappy voice.

Forget that world of crystal meth, Mary Jane and melting walls
You will never again venture down those nightmarish halls.
It is the dawn of a new day for you to walk into.
It is time you saw yourself. It is time you met you.

Remember who you are a scrapper bitch.
To some you will be more than you can ever know.
Hate to tell you this kid, though you have a way to go
To some girl, you are already a hero.

FAITH

Faith

Your mother knelt down
At the rail
To ask God to spare your life,
And 23 years later
God has made you someone's wife.
You said you never doubted,
Through the pain and all the tears,
And you chastised all your family
When they gave into their fears.
So where is your faith now, my dear
When you face this latest pain?
Why can't you lay your burden down
And keep prayers on your aim?
Why can't you
Who were a pillar,
No longer stand up tall
In your faith that God is with you
And will carry you through all?

Faith

It is the answer found in the black of night
To questions asked by the longing soul.
It brings inspiration to the crying heart,
Answering the yearning found deep within all.
Whether it is the Christian, Muslim, Jewish,
Or Hindu path or another divine way you follow.
As an endless wall, it protects and separates,
Giving comfort to some and causing wars.
Found within the pages of the Bible and Qu'ran.
On the ark when it came to rest on Mount Ararat.
The final sacrifice made by the martyrs of Mesada.
The question asked by the Son at Gethsemane
Older than the universe or planet Earth.
It is younger than man at his birth.
Whether in a church, mosque,
Temple or synagogue you worship.
Shrouded in ancient rituals and mysteries old,
Obscured by legends and language.
No matter to what Supreme Being
You kneel down to and pray,
After thousands of years
The question remains the same:
In what do you believe?

DREAMS

Daydreamer

"One o'clock and all is well!"
The young boy knew he was to yell,
But one o'clock and all alone
The little boy wished he were gone.

Off to dream in other lands.
Off to play on other sands.
But dreams are not that easy to find.
They warp and fade in the sands of time.

Life wages battle to take them away
The game of survival to ruin your play.

Things in life make us dance
Things in life make us weep.
But dreams are the best
And all we can keep.

Realm of Dreams

Scholar
Poet
Soldier
King

I am one and all these things.
I am the hero of which the birds sing.
I live in pages and glories old;
Told, retold growing ever bold.

Where the hero wins, the princess to wed,
Dragon slain, the evil villain dead;
A life sacrificed, the kingdom saved.
One saga ends, giving birth to a new age.

I am Long John Silver, Sherlock Holmes, and Sir Ivanhoe.
I am all these characters and more that you have yet to know.
Through rainy April days turning into gray November
I am that realm of dreams remembered.

I am Spiderman, Batman and the Man of Steel.
I live in comics and movies reel to reel.
I battle the Green Goblin, Joker, and Lex Luthor.
I am the adventures awaiting you in the bookstore.

Children at play skin their hearts and knees.
They learn to say thank you and please.
Games they play teach them to live, love and thrive.
They learn to give, share and never lie.

As they read each adventure, each book anew,
With the Hardy Boys, Dana Girls and, yes, even Nancy Drew,
They solved mysteries with these young sleuths,
Uncovered secrets and searched for clues.

As time will childhood can never last.
Childs's play and heroes are left in the past.
Becoming parents it is off to work they go,
Watching their children play, learn and grow.

With their children asleep snug in their beds.
Tired parents lie down and rest their weary heads.
They dream of that realm a night's sleep away,
Where once again as children they can play. . .

In
the
Realm
of
Dreams

PASSION

Charade

Your kisses sank into my thirsty skin
Like water in the desert heat,
But you did not know,
'Cause I hid my eyes from you
Hid my sighs from you
And opened my thighs to you only
After what appeared to be a long thought
Lest you know your power over me--
That I could not be
Doing anything else in this moment
Of my own free will.
My body aching for a drink of you,
Not just a sip or two,
With cries, and sighs,
And little lies
To conceal how good you feel.
To defend my charade.
So you may believe
That I am the taker
And you are the taken.

Payback

Clothes are a tangled mass on the floor,
My prisoner bound and held as never before.
My probing fingers caress your small breasts,
Seeking mouth on each nipple coming to rest
Feeding and nursing urgently until you moan;
First a primal hiss rising to a pleasured groan.
A trail of soft kisses across flat stomach's plane
Hands journeying through your tangled curly mane
Spread wide your legs and let me kiss your thighs
Until from your lips spill those soft innocent sighs
As I first nip, then tongue my way into your trove
As over your perfect bottom my exploring fingers rove.
My tongue curls around that splendid pink pearl
The torture begins as I send your senses awhirl
You plead, you cry, you beg, urging me to cease
My prisoner, only I can give that much needed release
From the secret passion fire burning deep, deep within
My lashing tongue shows no sympathy without end
"Yes, yes, yes." You hiss tossing and lost enraptured
You are my butterfly in amber, enamored and captured.
The tempo I quicken as your body responds and spasms
Harder my tongue and fingers probe, bringing the first orgasm.
That rips through your being bringing tiny tingling pleasures
Delving, biting and teasing I increase the growing pressure
I have only begun to torture you, my heart's prisoner I so adore.
Trembling you feel, my attentions demanding more explosions
"I love you," you scream, riding the torrent of released emotions.
I love the power I feel when I get to scratch that most wonderful itch
I gasp in delight as I feel expert, manicured fingers grip me below.
I moan as you sink to your knees, hand moving in that way only you
know.
Playfully teasing my earlobe, you whisper: "Payback is such a bitch!"

FORGIVENESS

What Does Forgiveness Feel Like?

What does forgiveness feel like?
Can I hold it here
Soft and warm, inviting
Or does it burn a cold fire
As devastating as the hateful blaze I fight?

What does forgiveness feel like?
Does it carry my burden to ease me
Or is it like matter—
The bulk neither created nor destroyed
Merely shifted
From the back to the head, to the heart?

What does forgiveness feel like?
And where to find it?
It's rarely advertised
By anyone but those guys on t.v.
With the tall hair
That never seem to open their eyes
When they speak,
Seeking forgiveness from Another.

I seek my own to dispense,
But I can't give what I don't have,
And I can't have what I don't know.
And so, I ask
What does forgiveness feel like?

Can You Forgive Me?

Can you forgive me?

I didn't mean to make you cry.
I didn't want to go there.
Your trust I did not mean to lose
Can't you see how much I care?

Can you forgive me?

I'm so tired of all these lies.
Can't you see and feel my pain?
Without you I wither and blow away
Only you can drive me this insane.

Can you forgive me?

I need you to hold me when I'm lost.
You know you are my whole world;
Without you I just can't breath.
For me there is only you, girl.

Can you forgive me?

I only looked at the menu, I did not order fun.
I am lost and do not know what I feel.
In this world you are the only one
That can makes my senses reel.

Can you forgive me?

Awakening to the ghost of your fragrance, alone,
I miss your clothes spread all over my floor.
So quiet and empty, this house is no longer home.
How loud was the final slamming of the door?

Can you forgive me?

Now, I know the true meaning of torment;
Without you, my life has no joy.
You were my angel hell sent.
Come back to me please?

And
forgive
me.

FEAR

Journey

I walk alone this journey
That I cannot comprehend
The how's and why's and wherefores
Nor can I see the end.

Each day is fighting blindly
With the terror in my eyes
That behold, however aptly,
My fantasy demise.

The tale they tell is fiction,
Or so I pray at night;
Exposed as utter liars
In the wisdom of daylight.

Yet, what if it isn't fiction,
But more biography?
My terror eyes foretelling
The history of me?

Dementia

Who was that?

The Little People, who live in the cabinet under the sink, laughing and
dancing their jig.

Was I here yesterday?

The child with eyes dark and eternal stares out unseeing, reaching her
hand for mine, reaching for my soul.

Am I here now?

The prick of the Soul Sewer's needle passing in and out, in and out of
my flesh, the thread pulled through my veins as I am neatly stitched
into a pattern I cannot comprehend.

Will I be here tomorrow?
Someone I do not know stands here in my place, wearing my face.

Where am I now?
The Armageddon rages all around!
The angels above bid me join their glorious host.
The devils below in harsh whispers list the torments I am to suffer.

What do they want with me?
Suddenly I can hear them all whispering to me:
"Tell us! Tell us! What do you fear?"
I
scream into the maddening chaos:
"No! Be silent. Leave me alone."

My eyes open wide. I am awake.
All is blissfully still. There are no voices in my head.

In this new dawn, I smile, for I have met my fear
And it will trouble me no more.

SORROW

Blue

Colors fade
Bright greens, soft grays give way
To the overwhelming blue.
No rose-colored glass detracts
From this all-consuming hue
The deep dark blue
Where it once lay beating
Red with life
Now blue with strife
And grief and pain
The deep blue stain
Remains, untouched by other colors.
Yellows, oranges, reds betrayed
To the overwhelming blue.

Red

The setting sun
Rose among thorns
A shattered promise
A heart broken in two
Lips sharing one last kiss
Eyes swollen from crying
Blood flowing from the wrist
The message light on the machine
Ambulance running a hopeless race
The flames of the candles in the chapel
Carnations thrown onto the lowered casket
The cold reality of what has been lost
Never
to
be
found
again.

LONELINESS

Alone

Alone
A stranger in a strange place
A home that isn't home
And a room that's not my own.

Alone
All faces unfamiliar
All surroundings new
And I recognize so few

Alone
And no one cares
And no one reaches out
And no one notices

Alone
All courtesies are forgotten
All eyes are turned away
Are people really so afraid?

Alone
I am, and so I stay
And wonder
Am I the victim of some destiny?

And if I am
Are all my days
Arcing toward some cosmic end
Alone?

Invisible

A vacant smile, half a nod, a role I assume.
As I stand in the center of a crowded room
A façade that I wear because it is expected
Of cool poise, charm when life is so hectic.
Can you see past this mask to the real me?
I'm right here; would it help if I screamed?
I am a man for too short a season.
I am thought without reason.
I am cause with no affect
Am I so easy to forget?
A poem with no rhyme
I am lost in time
I am one,
Invisible.

WRITER'S BLOCK

The Unwritten Ache

There lingers upon my heart
An unwritten ache I cannot mend.
My usual medicines have no effect
On that tender point of my heart.

No verses can end the suffering.
No rhyme a balm to my aching soul.
No metaphor captures
The full force of my sorrow-darkened heart.

Of all life's sufferings,
I've had not one affliction
Uneased by pen and word
'Til now.

When the words in my heart
No longer find the page
And my grief lies unabated
Smoldering.
And I pray
Someday
I can write about you.

Addiction

The sweet ebb and flow ebb and flow.
Across the white expanse the words go.
Get out, get out, get out of my head!
Please let me return to my warm bed.

The words come and rhyme
Writing themselves in my mind
Until I have to give them, their release
To grant my poet's soul some peace!

It is a cancer, slow death, to experience life as I do.
Feeling society's meter and rhyme in all the season's hues.
Lost and swept away on this timeless ocean.
There is no compass to guide me through this storm of emotion.

The surf pounds in my heart, it sounds in my head.
Lines and rhymes spilling forth to the paper altar are fed.
Words that beg to draw their first breath from my pen.
Some call it a gift, some call it art, me, I call it a sin.

At night while all others sleep, there come the dreams
Lost in the world that is and the world that seems,
The words come to me in a river of black on white.
Drowning in darkness, I strike for the surface and fight

For the release that only putting pen to paper can achieve.
Ebb and flow, ebb and flow, yes please, please leave me!
It is the fire that leaves my heart, spirit and soul burning.
It is the kiss, my lover's caress, for which I am yearning.

If you do not write, but only read and pause to ponder
The highs, the lows, the ebb and flow of endless wonders
That are there written in the book you hold in your hands
Then who am I, Gentle Reader, to ask you to understand?

What you hold is beyond all measure of time and space
There is no wealth, no treasure that can ever fill its place.
Once the pen has traveled this path, it can never do so again.
The muse whispers inspiration from poem's first line to end.

Into the waiting poet's ear, feeding his need, his addiction,
Seducing from him or her poems, sonnets and other fiction
That reaches deep into the human heart to touch and it hold.
What you have there, Gentle Reader, is no more than my soul.

COUSINS

Michael

I never asked God for a brother,
So instead He sent me you,
My bratty brother-cousin
My mother's sister's son.

Somehow you crossed the chasm
That had defined our family tree
To become my steadfast supporter
My shoulder to cry on.

You re-entered my life in a time of need.
You sat at my sickbed
And reminded me I was still here
And became my drier of tears
My ear to bend.

Then you left me again
To defend us all
My heart swelling with pride
Amidst the fear

'Til God returned you to me
And once again you became
My court jester
My wise sage
My psychoanalyst
My counsel
And my best friend.

Alison

My dear cousin Alison
Is my critic, my shrink, and my friend.
With poet's wit and charm,
She can a crowd of patrons disarm.
Then with her prose, meter and style
She keeps them laughing all the while.
This tiny tower of literary strength,
Her infinite heart and spirit are beyond all length.
Her ready grin and wry wit never waver,
She is a woman for all seasons in so many flavors
Her culinary skills know absolutely no end.
But help us men Lord, when her muse descends.
Smiling, she will hand us the menu for Dominos.
Because reaching for the phone, we grumble and know
This translates into: Boys, order out, we're dining in.

INSECURITY

If I Were Pretty

If I were pretty,
I would not be alone,
Sitting here waiting
For life to go by
Listening to friends
Of everyone else
Taking for granted
All I desire.

If I were pretty
No one would say
"Well, she's got a nice face...
Great personality."
Compliment and insult in a single line,
Because it's everything good,
But nothing you want.

If I were pretty
If I didn't were glasses,
Plus-sizes, retainer
If the diets had worked—
Diet shakes, diet pills,
Even dangerous ones.
If the surgery didn't cost so much.

If my hair wasn't brown, but blond,
Maybe red...
Or maybe if my eyes were blue.

If everything that shouldn't matter
But does
Could be changed—
If I were pretty
Maybe then you could see me.

Mr. Insecurity

(Thought processes running through the male mind at a party)

Hi there, can any of you absolutely beautiful women see me?
Right, over here hidden by the potted palm, that's me, Mr. Insecurity.
I stand here trying to look all assured, confident and cool.
Well women here is the 4-1-1, with film at 11,
I have no game, am not smooth and I am certainly no Tom Cruise.
So many beautiful women I only wish to adore.
God my confidence has locked itself in the john! Which way is the
door?
I come to these parties to see women that I will never know.
Oh how fragile is that poor creature the male ego.
Women are so lucky. They're not slaves of the male sex drive.
Look at her! Long black hair, delicious legs tucked in a skin-tight
black skirt.
Lips smiling, her smoldering eyes scan the room, like a huntress after
her prey.
Wait a minute. Is she motioning toward me? No, don't look. Ok now
look. Oh shit she is!
Danger, Will Robinson! Danger! Hide! Hide! Dive! Dive!
Wait are those her Prada clicking across the floor?
Why do I feel so trapped, so freaked out, so afraid?
Please, Lord, shoot me! At this rate I will never get laid.
Cool, OK she passed me by. Oh that was close.
Now I just got to crawl out of here. Wait? What is that tapping
sound?
Quick, beam me up, Scotty!

"Why are you back there?" I hear a thick Russian accent ask. "Are you
hiding from me?"
Caught, I smell the scents of roses, oils and cloves.
Why do I torture myself, only God knows.
"I-I-I." OK, calm down, play it cool and swallow. "No way, would I
be hiding from you.
Could you excuse me, I have to go to the bathroom."

Oh yeah that's me. Mr. Insecurity

HONOR

Crucified by Fire

Dedicated to the brave men and women who died at the World Trade Center and continue to avenge our nation in the Middle East.

Crucified by fire, you died
That others might survive.
You sank into your steely grave
With ne're a thought of giving up.

And crucified by fire,
Still you die for me.
And my children, so that they
May know a life of joy,
So fearless and so free.

So come home my gentle soldiers.
Come home to rest at last,
Where you need not fear your fellow man,
Or heed the fiery blast.

The war may not be over,
But the victory is sure.
For the sacrifices made today
Are of those whose hearts are pure.

So come home my gentle soldiers
And put your souls to rest
And know the nation understands
You did your ever best.

A Father's Love

For my father

A silent vigil, he stood alone among the head rows in the garden of stone.
His scarred face wet with tears lost in the rain.
A sentinel lost in the endless void of pain,
A storm raged within and without.
He stood guardian over his sleeping child.
"My son, my son." He repeated all the while.

You were so small, so perfect in form
My boy, I held you when you were born.
I looked into your beautiful eyes and said:
"You are my son, rest your weary head."

Where are you now?

I was not there for your first Christmas.
I missed your making your first birthday wish.
I was away when you lost your first tooth.
I held and cried with you when we lost Old Ruff.

We shared the bliss of your very first kiss.
We shared the ache of that first broken heart.
No my son I told you, it was not the world's end, only the start.
As your sister taught you to dance, I cheered.
I remember when we shared our first beer.
We spoke of secret things your mother would never understand.
Day by day, I was awed by the simple miracle as you grew from boy to man.

Where are you now?

When you enlisted you knew I would not approve.
A doctor, a lawyer is what I wanted for you.
I remember the angry words we exchanged before you left for Iraq.
I read of the seven lives you saved in the mortar attack.
The Medal of Honor to you they bestowed.
I love you so, my son the hero.

Where are you now? My son, my son.
I pray that you are never again, alone.

75

ANGER

Firestorm

When you see the firestorm brewing
Behind my clouded eyes,
Don't ask me how I'm doing
For you're getting only lies.

When you see the teardrops falling,
The ones I can not hide,
You'll know I'm trying not to hurt you
As I slowly die inside.

But that's the choice that I am making
To hide it all within my heart,
Standing strong within my silence,
As I slowly fall apart.

This I do because I love you
And I want more for your life
Taking all your pain inside myself
And standing by you through your life.

Flashpoint

Words spoken in the heat of the moment;
Blows struck when words fail us both
Two volcanoes erupt, to spew forth their venom
To hurt each other anew with heedless abandon.
Wounds that fester and bleed down through the years
Never forgotten, never allowed to heal.
Old hurts and insults that sting long after the cause is forgotten,
Drowned in tears that are never allowed to fall.

Until. . .

One falls silent in eternal slumber
One is left with alone with silent regret.

PERSONAL HEROES

The Walk of Fame

Scattered stars upon the ground
In a long and winding
Path to nowhere.
And people follow
And stand in awe
Of scattered stars
And give each star a name.
These pilgrims come
To the see the magical place
Where the stars have been humbled
To the ground for men
To tread upon.
More pilgrims come to the siren song,
"Come write your name upon a star!"
With no sense of their destiny
To be trod upon
By mortal feet.

Soldiers

They are the first to always answer their nation's call,
No matter how many of their comrades will fall.
They come in every American creed and hue;
Black, white, red, yellow, there are never too few.

They call each other: "My sister, my brother
'Cause when the bullets are flying, all they got is each other
Doing something they each know beyond question is right
Since 4 July 1776, never yielding in battle they fight.

When there is no one there, to tell them the reasons why,
They joined up, drilled and deployed, risking their lives.
Alone, each stands a sentinel in the coming Iraqi dawn.
Never are they truly alone, those of the Force of One.

There is always a hand to lift each to the higher ground.
By codes of honor, trust and fidelity are each to the other bound.
They live a way of life that no civilian can ever comprehend.
Not for a paycheck, travel or personal glory, our nation they defend.

Soldiers are possessed of personal courage, both moral and strong.
In war's fury, it guides them to always know right from wrong.
So sleep in peace America under the blanket of freedom they provide
When sent somewhere to defend, the pledge, the idea and your way
of life

So America, when a soldier in uniform you see, tell him or her:
"Thank you."
For wearing an ACU or carrying an M16 and doing all they do.
Because it is them and not you, individually doing what they can.
They are the last line of defense and blood shed in Iraq's sands.

Why this tribute to your sons and daughters, these heroes bold?
Because I am one, and there are so many that I know.

JOY

Where is My Joy?

I can see joy in another.
I can see it all the time.
The light shines from his face, or hers
Like something of the Divine.

I can hear joy in another—
Her voice carries a song
Every sentence sung in melody
So her heart can sing along.

I can see joy on their faces.
I can hear joy in their songs
What grips my heart in utter grief
Is I cannot sing along.

I can find joy anywhere I look
I can find his, hers, or thine.
Yet no matter where I look
I still cannot find mine.

Joy is...

Joy is waking up with you safe in my arms.
Joy is making love in a lightning-filled storm.
Joy is gazing at the moon and stars beyond mortal reach.
Joy is walking hand in hand, barefoot down a moonlit beach.

Joy is walking together getting soaked in the rain.
Joy is the shower and wine we share to get warm again.
Joy is feeling the rhythm of the city beat in the August heat.
Joy is a ferry ride around Ellis Island, seeing Lady Liberty.

Joy is the water fight we have instead of washing the car.
Joy is weekends, lost in each other, the world away so far.
Joy is cuddling together in the hammock for an afternoon nap.
Joy is backpacking in autumn, with you misreading the map.

Joy is cuddling on the couch, fighting over who controls the remote.
Joy is you teaching me to cook never bitching when I break the yolk.
Joy is sharing cotton candy when stuck on the Ferris wheel for an
hour.
Joy is the two of us surrendering at night to passion's infinite power.

Joy is fajitas and the margaritas we mix at home in the blender.
Joy is your scent on my clothes and how many days it lingers.
Joy is kisses shared under a blanket during a Dallas Cowboys game.
Joy is the simple bliss that you bring into my life again and again.

Joy is the smile on your face when coming home, finding me there
first.
Joy is the kiss we share, stripping as we feed our hunger and thirst.
Joy is each caress; each kiss; each nip and scratch as two become one.
Joy is the secret realm we share, only for us two, that is our very own.

PRIDE

Icarus

Written in the aftermath of Sept 11th

My God, were we Icarus
Chasing the sun?
Had we gotten so mighty
You melted our wings?

We've walked the stars
We've mined the moon
But we never would have thought
We had threatened the heavens.

Now we are humbled in our grief.

Is Pride Really a Sin?

Sages warn us that it always goes before the fall.
They say that pride is man's greatest sin and fault.
They say it is the most deceptive among the original seven.
To this which we accept as truth, I must ask why my friend?

Where is the sin in. . .

A father's pride the first time he holds his infant son?
A mother's proud tears, as her daughter in white linen, vows do ex-
change?
A boy's pride after sliding home, the baseball game won?
A girl's glee and pride on that first bike ride, without training wheels?
Parent's pride as they watch their child's first steps taken?
Grandparent's pride when they teach their granddaughter to tell time?
A poet's pride when his poetry inspires others to live and explore?
An artist's pride, upon hearing others tell him what his art has meant
to them?

How proud are we each when against all odds we succeed?
Where is the sin that sages warn us so zealously against?
The answer is found only when pride becomes vanity.

COURAGE

Her Silent Killer

For Patricia Patton, beloved teacher

She had survived
She'd somehow struggled through
Those years in which her silent killer
Stealthily stalked her weakening body.
She'd regained life and done the things
that made her life worth living...

Until it came again.
As sneakily silent as before,
It crept in stealthily in the night
To seize her body once again
And wake her from her fantasy
To face her living nightmare.

Still she kept on.
Nothing held her back.
She took her chemo with her.
Doctors said, "stop working"; she would not.
Nothing held her back.
She faced her killer with all the fight she could muster.
We never saw her cry.

She prayed to God and held on to her faith.
More than I could always do in times of strife.
She prayed for a miracle.
She was one.

Is there not one small miracle for such a miracle to grasp?
Some say life is a miracle.
If so, then what is death?
How many times does she ask that of her silent killer
As it laughs and takes her place?
Why did nothing hold it back?

The Standard Bearer

The 2nd Texas Infantry was entrenched, their sharpshooters waiting
and ready.
The stalwart 99th Illinois advanced toward the Confederate positions.
Volley after volley did the 2nd Texas sharpshooters fire into their
midst.
Though many Union soldiers fell, their courage refused to yield.
From this smoking and screaming hell, one lone figure emerged and
marched on.
The Texans sent two more volleys whistling into the Union line.
Bathed in the blood of his brothers, still he did not miss a step.

Sergeant Tommy Higgins advanced at the center of the diminishing
line of infantry.
His dry mouth tasted of ash, the battle field stank of sweat and
death.
The standard he held high, fluttering on the hot April wind for all to
see
He was so young when the war began, now he felt so old and bone
weary.

The young sergeant marched through the horror that rained down
upon Vicksburg.
He saw brother fight brother, fathers cut down their sons, all answer-
ing duty's call.
The young nation torn asunder, cried for its children, Bill Yank and
Johnny Reb.
In the hellish chaos of 22 May 1863, a miracle was witnessed by all.

The honor of those fallen that day, the standard bearer carried
proudly onward.
To a man the war weary Confederates stopped and stared at the awe-
inspiring sight.
"Do not shoot that man!" the Texans shouted down the line, hats off
in salute.
A hundred enemy hands reached down to pull the mud-splattered
sergeant up over the parapet.

His hand they shook one and all, as a thousand Confederate hats flew
into the air

95

Cheers of "Huzzah! Huzzah!" and "Damned stubborn yankee!" rang
out.
Though enemies in war they might be, as men the Texans admired
the courage of Sergeant Tommy Higgins.

A year after the war's end, when once again South and North greeted
each other:
As father to son, brother to brother and friend to friend, war wounds
healed
Based in no small part on the testimony of hundreds of Texans, who
carried the tale from Austin to New Orleans to Washington.
For his gallantry to Sergeant Higgins the Medal of Honor was bestowed.

GROWTH

Life's Path

A boy is born with childish dreams.
To him they do not seem to be.
The boy grows up, becomes a man,
But now can't dream
Like young boys can.
A man grows old, and sometimes dim,
But finds that he can dream again.

Turning Point

I was lost and could find no way out.
Tired I was of being only an afterthought.
I went to the mountains to be alone and die.
I was done living all these half-truths and lies.

No longer, would I be the oh-so-perfect-son.
Soul weary, being empty, I rested on a jagged throne.
Always at odds or out of place, nowhere do I call home.
I paused to savor the splendor of an eagle soaring on the wind.
Kneeling there, I prayed: "Lord grant me peace and final end."

A searing gust 'cross the mountain blew me toward that finite edge.
On this hellish zephyr, a booming voice commanded simply, "Jump."
Dazed, I prepared to obey, taking that faithful leap to my sufferings
end.
With the scents of roses, there came a cool, caressing air holding me
fast.

"Michael, listen not." A thousand voices whispered to me from the
vast.
Serenity filled my troubled soul, allowing me to see me and the world
anew.
One last message I heard: "My son, you must live. Your life has only
begun."
Tears I so longed to shed I cried there, listening to the singing upon
the wind.

That day, I learned to be myself and I took from the mountain one
final lesson.
No matter where in life I walk, I never walk alone.

PETS

Grey Boy

Softly now you nuzzle me
My handsome baby boy
With your gray coat slicked,
Pristine white chest,
And your little white socks,
As though the world is always a bit too cold.
You curl up against me,
You fall fast asleep
And dream of a better world than I could.

My Furry Enemy

They say he is man's best friend
To me he will be my death and end.
He grins at me when no one is around
How I hate that leering hound.

He barks and carries on when we talk.
He jumps about when we go for a walk.
This dog wants to haul ass and run,
Dragging me along screaming, just for the fun.

Wherever I am, he just has to be.
Can't you figure it out, Frankie? Get away from me.
He'll sneak his head under my hand to be stroked and pet,
Licking my hand again and again, leaving it slobbery and wet.

Yuck! (Just look at him grinning at me.)

No, I did not stay up with him all night when he was sick.
I just couldn't get to sleep and happened to be up.
That Irish setter is a true rogue; he knows every trick.
When he was a wee thing, he was such a cute pup.

Where did that new chew toy come from?
How should I know? Hell no, I didn't buy it.
Will you all stop smirking oh-so-knowingly-at-me!
Just give it to him and let the blasted mutt try it.

I loathe him, but no matter how much I try to ignore
This four-legged, ham sandwich snatching thief,
He will snuggle up under my feet, and begin to snore.
It is only then I can relax with any sense of relief.

FRIENDS

Carolyn

I barely knew you really
But you shared so much of much of my life.
You knew every bad-boyfriend tale—
Things I never told another.
As though my secrets could be bound
In the acrid odor of perms and hairspray.

I always knew I could trust you.
You trusted me too.
So we shared stories—
Of romantic frustrations,
Of personal struggles,
Of illness and fear.

You kept my secrets
You took them to your grave.
And the world is a lesser place without you
Carolyn.

The One Always Th

The hand that lifts you to higher grou
When you are flat on your face and can't get u

The One always there

The joker who keeps battering at your blues until you smile;
Never leaves until he knows that you are okay.

The One always there

The one you call after you get the One, for the hundredth time
At 2 a.m., who listens and says, "You go guy, see you tomorrow."

The One always there

The fist that hits you square in the face and keeps punching at you
until
you are ready to strike back at the world and live again.

The One always there

The shoulder you cry on, that arms that hold you up when the
Loss of your father hits as he is lowered into the ground.

The One always there

His kids all call you "Uncle" and bum rush you when you enter the
door,
wrestling you down into a laughing tangle of arms and legs until you
give
in and take them to the zoo.

The One always there

When you have a fight again with your sister or brother,
He is the other who makes you understand that meaning of family.

The One always there

n you are lost in the eye of life's insane hurricane
no keeps you grounded and lets you find your way.

The One always there

.roughout the years no matter in what country you stand in
No matter what trouble you manage to get in.

This One is always there.

MYSELF

Definition

I'm the fat chick with glasses.
I'm the short brunette.
I'm the writer you can't comprehend.
I'm the rather young woman,
With a very old soul,
And more grit than most Hollywood stuntmen.
And the scars to prove it.
I'm the girl you whispered about.
The one you tried to define.
You want me inside the box,
And walking the line.
'Cause you understand the box, I know,
And the line is all you can see.
But it just goes to show
That maybe next time,
You should leave the defining to me.

Facets of Myself

"It's easy, Michael just be your self.
Such is the great advice my parents gave me.
No answer to the question did they provide.
What is the eternal question I ask each day?
Who am I? What is Michael? Do I matter?

I am an explorer, seeking new horizons
I am a soldier and warrior-poet
I am a writer, a scholar seeking truth
I am a lover without a love, who is lost.

I am good and evil, walking life's edge
I am passion and fury, a raging fire in the night
I am an hour with no glass walking time's sands
I am a glass half full, waiting to be shared by two

I am the journey's road not taken, not the destination end
I am young. I am old. I am a sage. I am a court jester and fool.
I am the hero around which sagas are retold again and again.
At one time or another, each role has defined a different me
As I defined each facet of myself.

I am this and that and much, much more.
Ah, but if you wish the simple truth
I am just a man.
I am myself.
I am me.

DEATH

Death Defeated

Death, you came in your most fearsome form—
With no black robe, skull head, or sickle.
You came quietly, invisible.
Never announcing your presence.
Never reaching out to touch.
Simply sitting silently,
And soaking up my life—
Like ice sapping heat from a room.
I felt your presence, but
Invisible and silent, you were impossible to fight.
But God sent me an angel
To shed light on you.
No longer invisible or silent,
You were reduced
To flesh, and blood, and bone—
And all in our control.
So we beat you this time,
The angels and I,
And I bask in your defeat—

Until you come again.

Light a Candle for Me

Will you light a candle for me?
Place it in the window so that I may see
My way home after so long a journey.
Aye, the end is so near it seems.

Please light a candle for me.

For a man who has met life's ups and downs,
A weary traveler who danced with Destiny,
One single taper burning for me.
A welcome beacon at the end of life's journey;
A reminder of a woman I left behind.
A lady of quality ever present in my mind.

Please light a candle for me.

I see that candle burning bright;
A tiny flame amid the black gloom of night.
To guide me home at the end after the battle won.
A fire in my heart that inspires me to fight on
When wounded and crimson bloody,
My weary, falling body
Struggles to lift the family standard high
To cradle it against my body as I die.

Please light a candle for me.
All this I long for
Lying here, dying here
A world away, remembering all.
Darkness beckons, not a dark angel of death.
Merely, an old friend, come bid me welcome
As I draw my last breath.
With the scents of the world all around
As my ears drink deep of the sounds that here abound.
As last peace and harmony has this soldier found.

Yes, light a candle for me!

DICHOTOMY

Dichotomy-A Woman's View

You are calm when I'm afraid.
Hot when I'm cold
Awake when I sleep.

You are well when I'm sick
But sick when I'm well
Hungry when I'm full
And stalwart when I weep.

You stand up when I fall
So I can stand for you too.
You defend me
So I defend you.

You think my cooking too salty
But yours is too bland
You prefer your new sports car
I, my well-worn old van.

I don't like you so messy.
You don't get when I clean.
You want soft browns and yellows.
I want bright blues and greens.

Forces incompatible
From opposed family trees.
Yet we somehow enmesh
Our dichotomy.

Dichotomy—A Man's Definition

I tell the boys: "Hell, yes" to guys-night-out.
You tell me: "Hell no." with an angry shout.
I want to stay home see the Cowboys play.
You want to drag me out to the ballet
I like a margarita with salt and lime
You won't even partake of a glass of wine.
I am up, packed and all ready to go
You want your first cup of coffee.
I want to make love and play
You want to roll over and sleep
I have a great day and want to share
Yours went bad; you're cross as a bear
I wake you with a tender hug and kiss
You tell me I need a breath mint and a shave
I got a new Mustang! Want to go for a ride.
You would rather walk, take a bus or fly.
I never can see eye to eye with you on anything
You enjoy our "discussions" heard four blocks away.
I just don't know why I'm here. Why together we stay.
You smile that knowing smile and remind me again.
Just how fun it can be to disagree.
God, I love this thing called dichotomy.